TRAMP

MALCOLM CARRICK

HARPER & ROW, PUBLISHERS
New York, Hagerstown, San Francisco, London

for ricky and natalie

First Edition

Library of Congress Cataloging in Publication Data
Carrick, Malcolm.
    Tramp.

    SUMMARY: A shy young boy befriends the tramp
who has invaded his special hideaway.
    [1. Tramps—Fiction. 2. London—Fiction]
I. Title.
PZ7.C23452Tr3   [E]   76-58723
ISBN 0-06-021117-2
ISBN 0-06-021118-0 lib. bdg.

TRAMP

1969712

IN the middle of smoky London Town, there was a grassy railway place. There the steam trains, billowing on their way to London Bridge, went under the road. If you leaned over the bridge when one passed, huge clouds of fresh white steam covered you like sheets. When it cleared, you could see St. Paul's. You could walk to St. Paul's from where we lived.

I liked playing in the long grass all by myself. There was a ditch there, and spiky hawthorn bushes grew around the railway signal pole that hummed.

It was better there than in the streets full of other kids' marbles and chalked pavements. Better than listening to the radio where adventures happened to other people, but not to me. Better than the playgrounds on the bomb sites, where gangs of kids picked on me.

In my grassy place, empty like the countryside in books, there was no one to say "Cat got your tongue?"

In my place, *I* made things happen. *I* made the hawthorn into Robin Hood's longbow. *I* made the phantom horse, Black Bess, come alive again. My Black Bess, who did whatever I wanted her to.

When the railway pole hummed loud and pulled its roots from the ground to become a giant stick monster who caught trains and princesses with her spidery lines, I fought her. I whacked her until she went back to being a pole.

Then I'd awaken the Princess with a kiss, like they do in the story and in the pantomime. The Princess was as pretty as Sally James, and she never laughed at my big ears like Sally did.

When Billy the Kid came to London to
shoot it out with the Queen, I drew my sword
on him. The Queen gave me a medal for that,
and a big hug.

No one came to my place then, except the
odd animal friend, or the lovers I giggled away.

10

Every day I played there, but not Sunday. Can't-go-out-to-play day. All of us, big brother Dick, little brother Dave, scratchy in Sunday best. Sitting in the parlor only used on Sunday and Christmas. Everything there smells of polish.

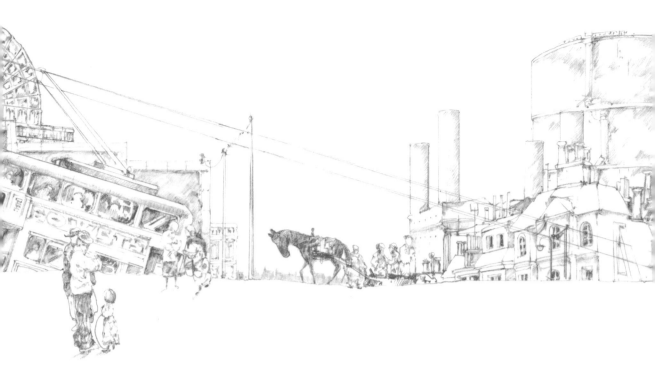

All the family walks to chapel. Outside, Dad
talks to Mr. James from across the road. Sally
James and her two ugly sisters, all in fluffy
white, make faces at me, giggling at my ears
sticking out from my new haircut, giggling be-
hind rows of red, grown-up hands clutching
Bibles.

Mr. James stares down at me.

Back home at the table, little brother starts singing "Sally, Sally, pride of our alley." Then they all start giggling into their dumplings, trying to make me cry, just because I told Dick I liked Sally. He told every giggling one. Don't cry, do something.

Knock off the plate, SMASH, onto the stone scullery floor. Dumplings dripping, gravy on Uncle's boots, quiet for a moment.

Leave me alone. I know dumplings cost money, I will clean his boots, the plate is only broken in three, Uncle Joe can stick it together again. Uneasy quiet now, Sunday's full of quiet, full of waiting.

15

At my place the next day, I declared war on everyone who ever stared or giggled at me, made me cry. They all gathered on the other side of the ditch. They grew a hundred times bigger, with long hairy noses, holding plates of gristly meat. "We'll make you eat this!" they jeered.

16

I shouted for Black Bess and drew my trusty longbow. With my war cry "For England and St. Paul's," I leapt up on Black Bess, together we charged into the ditch— "Oh."

There was someone in the ditch. He moved, dirty, old in a shapeless black coat. He mumbled at me. Tramp.

Run home quick, back to the streets full of uncles and aunts, back to the kitchen full of warm Mum.

"Didn't mean to break the plate, Mum."

"All right, luv, Joe'll fix it."

The next day, Tramp was still there, in *my* place. Dirty thoughts for dirty Tramp. "Go away—" The words shouted in my head but the cat had got my tongue and wouldn't let them out. So I had to send in my Royal troops . . . but they couldn't move him.

Back to the streets where the other kids played, but Black Bess couldn't roam free there.

Back to the radio, where other people had adventures, but not me.

Back to the playgrounds on the bomb sites, where princesses couldn't walk with the rough kids.

18

Back to my street, where they play ordinary games.

There's Lenny Smith's gang playing soccer. Careful, they're looking at me, they're staring, quick, say something, quick before they see you're scared. . . .

"I . . . I know where there's a tramp."

"Tell us," they said. I told them and they went to see him. I followed them. I saw them throw things at the tramp, sticks and stones, then big things, bricks. But the tramp didn't move.

21

Then *they* were scared, then Lenny Smith's
gang ran away.

Tramp was huddled up quite still. I went close
to him. His eyes opened, they looked at me. "It's
your fault," his eyes said. Then they closed.

Run home quick, back to the streets full of
uncles and aunts, back to the kitchen full of warm
Mum, back to the bed full of Brother. But don't
tell what happened. Tell-tale-tit, you told Lenny
Smith about Tramp.

Come quick, sleep; hurry up, morning. Lamplighter whistling, come on; milkman clinking and
clipping over the cobbles in the alley.

Hurry up, Dad's early morning coughing, I
must go back to see if Tramp is all right.

But I had to stay in, to wait for the rent-man.
It was late before I could get out, back to my
place.

Tramp hadn't moved. He was lying in the gathering dew, damp.

"Are you all right?" I asked from a long way away. He didn't answer.

Perhaps he was ill or . . . dead?

I called for Black Bess to ride him to the hospital, but she could only ride in games. There was only me there who could do anything. Only me there to help. I went closer, not breathing. He saw me then. I wanted to run but couldn't. I mustn't. I opened my mouth but no words came out. He touched his lips, he was telling me something. What? What was he telling me?

24

Look: Lamps are lit, evening fog is eating St. Paul's.

Listen: Pianos are jangling in the pubs; wooden wheels, the market stalls are closing.

Smell: Chips frying. Must be late. Run home quick.

In bed, hissing gaslight makes tramp shadows on the wall. What did tramps put in their mouths? Wine? Beer? Cigarettes? Medicine? I touched my lips like he did. . . .

"You still hungry?" Dick asks.

"What do tramps eat, Dick?"

"Anything, I suppose."

Hurry up, sleep.

Get into the kitchen early next day, before Mum makes up the fires. Pinch a sandwich from Dad's case, an apple from Brother's schoolbag, a piece of Mum's bread pudding, a bottle of Uncle's beer, all in a paper bag. Off, off to my place, through Waterman Lane Market, get the morning windfall tomatoes, give them a rub, good as new. Off, off to my place.

28

Tramp was lying still in the ditch. I put the bag near him, then I went right up to him, near the smell, funny smell. Black Bess doesn't smell. I touched him and ran away. I was brave then.

Back home at dinner time, I wasn't brave. Uncle couldn't find his beer. "Who's had it?"

Keep quiet.

We're sent to the pub to get another bottle. Noisy smoky pub, full of legs and jangling piano music.

"You ask, Dick." Dick's brave all the time.

"Mister, get us a bottle of beer for my Uncle Arthur?"

Back at home I jumped every time someone said food. They're all looking a bit sideways at me. Mum's getting the bread pudding out, she'll see . . . THUMP! on the kitchen door. It's Uncle Joe with the mended plate.

"Hello, hello," he laughs.

"Tell us a story, Uncle Joe."

"Tell us a joke, Joe."

Joe tells and talks and laughs while I scoop out some pudding for him so no one notices the hole.

30

Next day at my quiet grassy place, there were the paper bag and the beer bottle . . . empty. Tramp's eyes were open wide and he looked at me. My tummy had butterflies like when Mum went to get the bread pudding, but I wasn't scared now. Tramp had eaten the food, so he must be better. That made me feel better about telling Lenny Smith.

Tomorrow's Saturday—pocket-money day. Tomorrow I can *buy* food for Tramp, not have to pinch it. "Pay my way," like Dad always says.

Happy, warm in bed, singing downstairs, onions frying, friendly hissing gas. I know what to get Tramp: chips.

Chips. There's two Fish and Chips in our street—Joe's is best. "Fourpennyworth, please. And a pickled onion, please, Mister Joe." Smell the chips wrapped up in newspaper, salted and vinegared. Hot, hot for Tramp.

And medicine, Dad's cough medicine. Run before the chips get cold, back to my place. He's awake. I put the chips in front of him and sat over in the long grass.

"They're hot," I said, proud. He nodded and ate them with dirty fingers, then he half sat up, pointing at the medicine. "That's medicine, if you're ill," I told him. He chuckled into his chips, mumbling at me.

Every day I brought him something to eat. One day I brought a crab's claw from the shell-fish man. It cost five pence—chips only cost three pence—but he didn't eat the crab's claw. He liked chips best. He licked the crunchy bits off his beard.

"Were you in the war?" I asked. He had strappings around his feet like soldiers in the army, like Uncle John who wrote letters. He didn't answer. When Mum or Dick didn't answer a question, it meant they were cross or too busy for me or something. But Tramp wasn't cross or busy. So I just talked and it didn't matter if he didn't answer.

All that week and the next, Tramp stayed at my place. Sometimes I'd talk to him, tell him things. If he didn't want to listen, I would play with Black Bess. She didn't mind Tramp being there. Neither did I.

Sometimes I'd make him a person in one of my stories. Usually I made him King of all the Russias, because he had a beard. He just sat and stared and mumbled, and Black Bess and I played around him.

Once on Sunday, I crept out after chapel. I passed Sally James' house. She was at the window and saw me.

"Where are you going?" she asked. "To get your hair cut again?"

"To see my friend," I told her.

"I didn't think you had a friend," she said, not giggling.

"Well, I have." I went on, not feeling shy at all. I was going to *my* place to see *my* friend.

"Tramp, you can be the man in the Bible who got turned into a pillar of salt. Then you don't have to get up." He laughed. "Do you like me?" I asked. He didn't say no.

On Monday I went with chips for Tramp, but he wasn't in the ditch.

"Tramp?" I called out for him, but he wasn't in the grass, he wasn't in the hawthorn, he wasn't anywhere. He had gone.

I just stood, staring at the place where we had been playing only yesterday. After all those chips, after sharing all the things I'd told him, he'd gone without saying.

The chips in my hand got cold and greasy. I flung them over the railway. I hit the railway signal pole, shouted, "I don't care, I don't care, dirty tramp!"

Home. Run home quick, back to the streets
full of uncles and aunts, back to the kitchen full
of warm Mum, back to the clean washing smell.

"What's the matter?" they asked. Mum, Dad,
Uncle, Brothers.

42

"Nothing," I said. I don't care.

But I did care. I went back to my place later, late, when the warm golden fog was eating St. Paul's, when the evening lamplighter whistled, when the pub piano began to jangle. At my place, I closed my eyes and turned around, hoping he'd be there. He wasn't. I searched the long grass for a message, but I knew I wouldn't find one.

Tramp didn't come back the next day, or the day after . . . he never came back.

He could have been my best friend if he'd wanted. More best than any princess, more best than even Black Bess. No one else had played with us at my place, only Tramp.

He was the only friend I'd ever made by myself; now he had gone. "Why?" I wondered. Perhaps he thought I wasn't a good friend to have, perhaps he thought I was too shy?

"But I'm not shy, am I, Black Bess? And I *was* a good friend to have. I looked after Tramp with chips and stuff. I worried about him. I cared. I bet I'd make someone a good friend."

Wander back slowly home; not so shy.

Back to the streets; not too sad.

Lamps are lit.

It's warm when you remember friends like Tramp.

Warm like the kitchen full of Mum.

Warm like the yellow fog all wrapped around you like a blanket. Sally James came out of the fog. "Your mum's calling for you," Sally said. I smiled. "You'd better go home, Malcolm," Sally said.

"You coming too?" I asked. She didn't answer, but she came. Past the jangling piano pub, with its glowing, colored windows, through the deep yellow blanket we went back to our street.

"Where's your friend?" she asked.

"Gone away," I told her.

"Oh." She put out her hand and touched my arm as gently as a ladybird landing.

At the end of our street, my door was open. We could smell bacon frying through the thick, damp taste of the fog. "Perhaps your supper's ready," smiled Sally.

Someone was singing far away; it was a funny
wrapped-up sound. The street was waiting for me
and Sally, it looked peaceful . . . safe. Sally's door
opened too.

"Sally," I said, "do you like chips?"

48